Race to the Moon!

Based on the episodes
"Moonstruck, parts 1 and 2"

Ready-to-Read

Simon Spotlight
New York   London   Toronto   Sydney   New Delhi

SIMON SPOTLIGHT
An imprint of Simon & Schuster Children's Publishing Division
1230 Avenue of the Americas, New York, New York 10020
This Simon Spotlight edition July 2018
Adapted by Natalie Shaw from the series PJ Masks
For information about special discounts for bulk purchases, please contact Simon & Schuster Special Sales at 1-866-506-1949 or business@simonandschuster.com.
Manufactured in the United States of America 0518 LAK
10 9 8 7 6 5 4 3 2 1
ISBN 978-1-5344-2204-9 (hc)
ISBN 978-1-5344-2203-2 (pbk)
ISBN 978-1-5344-2205-6 (eBook)

Amaya, Greg, and Connor
are learning about the moon.
When the moon looks orange
it is called a harvest moon.

It will happen tonight!
Luna Girl will be up to
no good.

This looks like a job
for the PJ Masks!

Greg becomes Gekko!

Connor becomes Catboy!

Amaya becomes Owlette!

They are the PJ Masks!

Now Luna Girl can travel
to the moon.
The harvest moon makes her
Luna Magnet stronger!

She wants to find the
harvest moon crystal.
It will make her so strong
that no one can stop her!

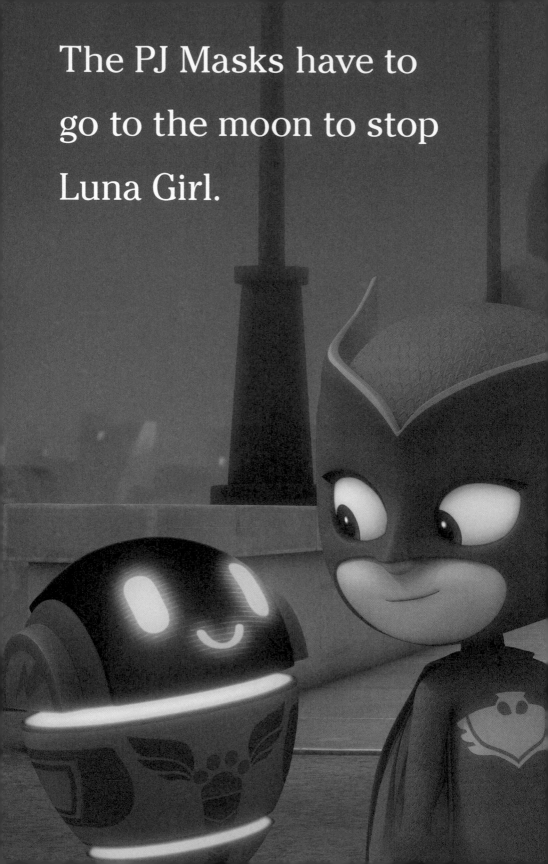

The PJ Masks have to go to the moon to stop Luna Girl.

PJ Robot can help.

He turns Headquarters
into a rocket ship!

PJ Masks are on their way
into space to save the day!

Then Luna Girl throws
energy bubbles at their ship.

Owlette tries to keep

the ship safe.

It does not work!

They have to land on
the moon.

Luna Girl is on the moon too!

The PJ Masks race out
on their PJ Rovers.

They are too late.

Luna Girl finds the

harvest moon crystal!

The PJ Masks have to
stop her!
Catboy tries to use
his Super Cat Speed.

It does not work!

Luna Girl laughs.

Their powers
do not work the same
on the moon.

Luna Girl uses the crystal
to make a trap
around the PJ Masks.

They escape
when Gekko uses his
Super Gekko Muscles!

The heroes break free
from the trap!

They work together to get
the harvest moon crystal.

The PJ Masks saved
the moon!